Text and illustrations copyright © 2019 by Benjamin Flouw

Tundra Books, an imprint of Penguin Random House Canada Young Readers, a division of Penguin Random House of Canada Limited

Library and Archives Canada Cataloguing in Publication

Title: Constellation of the deep / Benjamin Flouw.
Other titles: Constellis des profondeurs. English
Names: Flouw, Benjamin, 1986- author, illustrator.
Description: Translation of: Le constellis des profondeurs.
Identifiers: Canadiana (print) 20200210750 | Canadiana (ebook) 20200211684 | ISBN 9780735268968
   (hardcover) | ISBN 9780735268975 (EPUB)
Classification: LCC PZ7.1.F56 Con 2019 | DDC j843/.92—dc23

Published simultaneously in the United States of America by Tundra Books of Northern New York, an imprint of Penguin Random House Canada Young Readers, a division of Penguin Random House of Canada Limited

Originally published in 2019 by La Pastèque

Library of Congress Control Number: 2020936743

English edition edited by Peter Phillips
The artwork in this book is a mixture of digital painting and hand-painted textures.
The text was set in Linotte.

Printed and bound in China

www.penguinrandomhouse.ca

1   2   3   4   5   25   24   23   22   21

Penguin
Random House
TUNDRA BOOKS

ISTELLATION

OF THE

DEEP

Benjamin Flouw

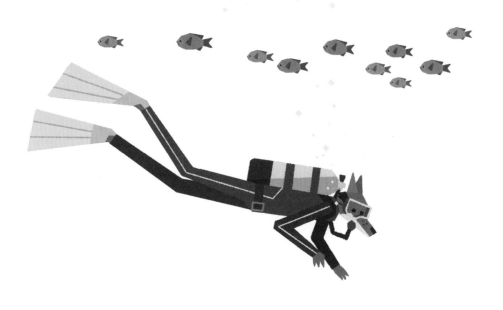

tundra

On summer mornings, Fox likes to walk the salty coastal trails.
Wolf, his cousin, often joins him.

"Fabulously fascinating!" exclaims Fox, pulling his head out of a leafy grove.

"What's fabulous," says Wolf, "is your fascination with strange plants!"

A loud seagull interrupts them. "Have you ever heard of the constellation of the deep? It's an amazing plant: it grows on the bottom of the ocean, but no one knows exactly where, and I've heard that it glows in the dark . . ."

Constellation of the deep! Fox's eyes light up. He's eager to get the diving equipment that Wolf keeps at home. He is careful not to forget anything:

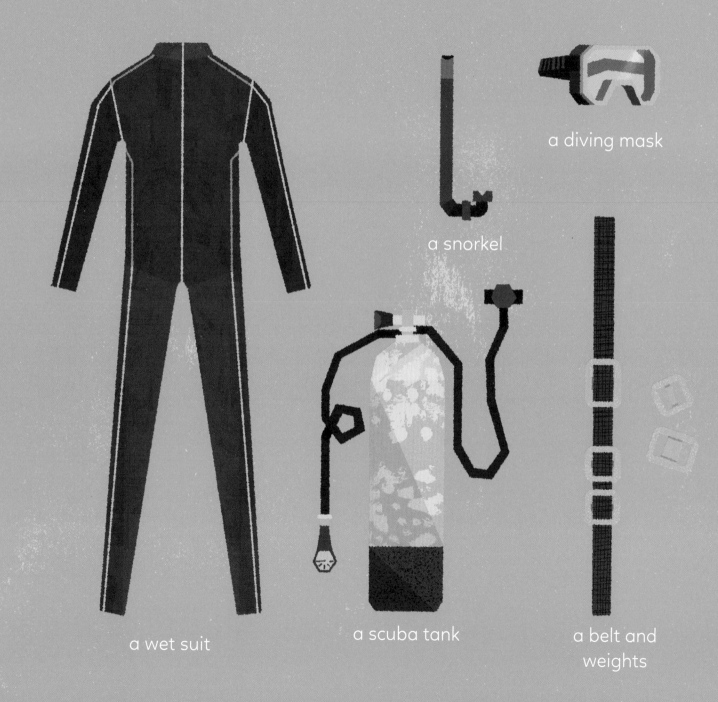

a diving mask

a snorkel

a wet suit

a scuba tank

a belt and weights

fins

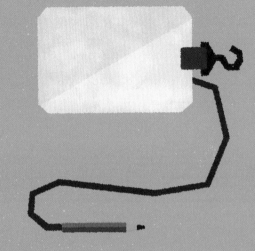

a slate and a pen that
writes underwater

a compass watch

a flashlight

and most important:
a camera to capture the discovery

While Fox gets ready and carefully enters the water,
Wolf observes the marine life at the edge of the ocean:

a saltwater crab

limpets

small blue mussels

a hermit crab

scallops

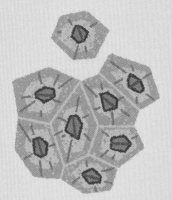

barnacles

periwinkles

a sea star

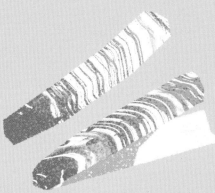

razor clams

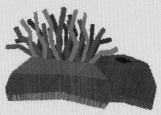

sea anemones

Meanwhile, Fox is already swimming among scorpion fish, conger eels and damselfish in the middle of a huge underwater meadow: a pasture of posidonia. Fox knows that posidonia are flowering plants, but they don't glow in the dark. He will have to explore the ocean more deeply . . .

To his amazement, Fox finds himself in the heart of a forest! Except that instead of being surrounded by trees, he swims among giant algae! Fox recognizes some of them . . .

eisenia

macrocystis

alaria

ecklonia

durvillea

laminaria

In the depths of this forest, Fox comes face-to-face with Otter.

"I'm looking for a fantastic plant that grows on the bottom of the ocean," Fox tells Otter. "It's said to glow in the dark."

"I discovered a place full of strange plants while I was looking for sea urchins the other day," says Otter. "You should take a look!"

Swimming through the leafy algae, Fox sees rocks covered with strange, multicolored sculptures. These aren't plants, but corals. They're so beautiful Fox has to stop and take a few photographs before he continues his search.

He marvels at the different shapes of corals:

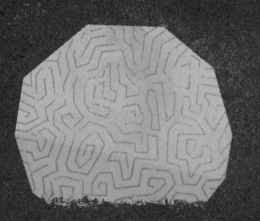

There are corals that look like brains,

trees,

long fingers

tables,

. . . and curled paper.

There are branching corals,

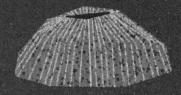

massive corals,

corals that look like elk horns

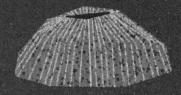

. . . and even mushroom-shaped corals.

But there's no sign of the constellation of the deep.

Fox needs help.

He asks small fish,

and bigger ones . . .

until, finally, Grouper agrees to help him.

Grouper takes Fox into the open water.
All they can see is blue.

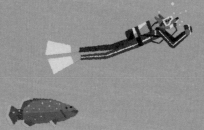

In the distance, a huge underwater mountain appears, surrounded by all kinds of fish.

Grouper leads Fox into a hole on the side of the mountain. At the bottom, something is glowing.

But it's only a tiny glowworm!

Of course, Fox still wants to take a photograph.
But oh no! His camera is gone!

From the edge of an underwater cliff, Fox looks into the abyss, all the way down to the bottom of the ocean. He does not have enough air in his tank. He won't discover the constellation of the deep today . . .

but what is that mysterious shape in the darkness?

It's Whale, who has returned
from hunting squid.

"You're in a bind, my friend. Let
me help you!" says Fox.

Fox struggles to remove the trash wrapped around Whale.
Between two cans and a plastic bottle, Fox miraculously
finds his camera.

To thank him, Whale helps Fox get back to the shore.

Fox returns, his quest unfinished, but it doesn't matter.
He has made some wonderful memories.

Back in Wolf's den, Fox shows his photos to his cousin.

"Look at this one. It's very beautiful," says Wolf, eating a grape pâté sandwich.

"That's it," exclaims Fox. "The constellation of the deep! My camera must have taken a photo when it touched the ocean floor!"

Fox pours himself a glass of mushroom juice. He is happy. He knows that every time he flips through his book of rare plants, the photo of the constellation will remind him of the fabulous beauty of the underwater world.